Megatron, leader of the Decepticons, is ruthless and cunning. He transforms from a gun to lead the Decepticons in their fight against the Autobots.

Soundwave transforms from a cassette recorder to a Decepticon communicator robot and acts as a radio link for the other Decepticons. He is able to read minds and will use blackmail for his own gain. Soundwave is despised by all other Decepticons.

Laserbeak is cowardly and will run for safety if he is threatened. He can fly at speeds of up to 250 mph and transforms from a spy cassette to the Decepticon interrogation robot.

Starscream transforms from a plane to the Decepticon air commander robot. He can fly faster than any of the Decepticons and seeks to replace Megatron as leader. Starscream is ruthless and cruel.

Rumble is small and tough. When he transforms from a spy cassette to the demolition robot, he transmits low frequency groundwaves to create powerful earthquakes.

Ravage likes to operate alone and is the craftiest of all Decepticons. He transforms from a spy cassette to a saboteur robot. He is very good at hiding himself in the shadows of the night and can walk without making a sound.

Once, long ago, a race of robot beings called Autobots were forced to wage war against another race of robots called Decepticons, to bring peace back to their home planet of Cybertron.

As the war went on, chance brought both sides to Earth. They crashed so violently on landing that all the robots lay in the Earth's crust, seemingly without life, for over four million years.

Suddenly the energy set in motion by a powerful volcanic eruption gives them life once more – and the war starts all over again here on Earth. Among the robots' many strange powers is the ability to transform into other shapes, and they use this to disguise themselves to fit in with the civilisation they find on Earth. The Autobots have to defend themselves, they have to protect this planet with all its valuable resources and the people who live here – and they must also build a new spaceship if they are ever to get back to Cybertron...

British Library Cataloguing in Publication Data

Grant, John

Laserbeak's fury.—(Transformers. Series 853; v. 4)
I. Title II. Collins, Mike III. Farmer, Mark IV. Series
823'.914[J] PZ7

ISBN 0-7214-0943-1

First edition

Published by Ladybird Books Ltd Loughborough Leicestershire UK
Ladybird Books Inc Lewiston Maine 04240 USA

written by JOHN GRANT

illustrated by MIKE COLLINS, MARK FARMER and STEVE WHITAKER

Ladybird Books

Megatron, leader of the Decepticons, wanted power. He wanted power over planet Earth so that he could return to his own planet Cybertron, and from there seize power over the entire Galaxy. But every time that power seemed within his grasp, he was foiled by the Autobots.

"It is unthinkable," he cried, "that I, the mighty Megatron, should be thwarted again and again by those fools and weaklings the Autobots!"

"Everyone has a weak spot," said Starscream. "Find the Autobots' weak spot and you have them in the palm of your hand."

"You may be right," said Megatron. "And I think I know what it is. The Earthlings who have befriended them...they mean a lot to Optimus Prime. We must find out all we can about these creatures."

"I say exterminate them," said Starscream. "This miserable planet would be all the better for being rid of those flabby human beings."

"What you say in unimportant!" cried Megatron. "Soundwave! Activate Laserbeak!"

"LASERBEAK . . . ACTIVATE!" said Soundwave. "OPERATION OBSERVE AND RECORD!"

An audio-cassette ejected from Soundwave's chest pack and transformed in mid-air to the ferocious bird-robot.

"Seek out Earth-people and observe them," ordered Megatron. "Locate one of their settlements. Study their habits. Transmit and record all that you learn."

In a moment the mechanical creature was winging its way swiftly through the sky.

"Study their habits!" laughed Starscream. "Do you want to become like them? Soft? You are too old, Megatron. It is time that the Decepticons had a new leader."

"I am old because I am hard," said Megatron. "An impatient fool like you, Starscream, will be lucky to survive to *half* my age."

Hidden in a remote area, the Decepticon base was far from the nearest town or village. The sun had set and the darkness was deepening over the countryside before Laserbeak saw the line of a road far below, and changed course to follow it. A moving light appeared. It was a car. Laserbeak swooped down for a better view. He signalled back to Megatron: "HUMAN VEHICLE ON HIGHWAY. PROCEEDING ONE TWO FOUR DEGREES. SPEED SEVENTY TWO KILOMETRES PER HOUR. OBSERVATION CONTINUES."

Megatron listened to the message.

"VEHICLE APPROACHING BUILDING COMPLEX. REDUCING SPEED. STOPPED. HUMANOID PASSENGERS EMERGING."

Laserbeak circled the farm as the farmer and his family got out of the car. A short distance away were other buildings: a village. On a hill the robot saw a tall tower-like structure with four outstretched arms. He flew towards it, signalling: "INVESTIGATING UNIDENTIFIED OBJECT..."

And at that moment he hit the overhead powerlines to the farm!

As the metal bird sliced through the high voltage cables, there was a blinding flash. The sudden shock caused a malfunction in Laserbeak's mechanism. He transformed in an instant to his cassette form and dropped to the ground. In the grass he tried desperately to transform back, but the electricity had temporarily de-energised his transformer unit.

The farmer ran towards the power line. Broken cables trailed uselessly on the ground and the lights and power in the farmhouse were dead. He lit an oil lamp and made his way to the telephone to report the damage. The engineer asked if he had any idea what could have been the cause.

"You probably think this is crazy," he said, "but just before the flash, I thought I saw something fly over the car. Like a big bird. The headlights reflected off it as if it were metal!"

Meanwhile, back at the Decepticon base, Megatron raged as Laserbeak's message was abruptly cut off. Soundwave re-adjusted the controls on the audio-monitor, but there was no response.

"Perhaps Laserbeak has been destroyed by the Earthlings," suggested Skywarp.

"Such a thing is far beyond their skill," said Starscream. "It is a temporary malfunction of his transmitting equipment. Keep trying, Soundwave."

Soundwave continued to adjust the controls.

"Suggest re-run and analysis of non-verbal signals," he said.

"Carry on, Soundwave," said Megatron.

Soundwave re-ran the tape of readings from Laserbeak's instruments. "AT THE MOMENT OF CUT-OFF LASERBEAK REPORTED UNKNOWN STRUCTURE. RADAR READ-OUT CONFIRMS. OBJECT IS MECHANICAL, BUT WITH ZERO MAGNETIC RESPONSE."

"Impossible," cried Starscream. "Such a mechanism cannot exist!"

"Nonetheless," said Megatron, "we will investigate."

While Megatron and the Decepticons puzzled over Laserbeak's interrupted signal, the Autobots were also mystified. Hound had picked up the signals and Optimus Prime called for Spike.

"I don't like it," said the Autobot leader, "when the Decepticons get so interested in the doings of the Earth people. I don't think that they're planning to do them any favours. Spike, what do you make of all this?"

Spike shook his head. "Not much," he said. "Laserbeak evidently followed a car to a small town or village. He saw something on a hill. Radar, do you think?"

"A Decepticon would recognise and understand a radar installation," said Optimus Prime. "Hound, can you fix Laserbeak's last known position from the signals?" He fetched a map, and while Hound read out the figures he said, "Here it is: a small village lying among the woods and hills."

"Right," said Optimus Prime. "Hound, go and investigate. Spike had better go too. Perhaps he can explain what it was Laserbeak saw."

Shortly after daybreak the engineers arrived at the farm to repair the broken power lines. As they got down from their truck they looked at the severed cables.

"Wow!" said one. "Would you look at that! And this farmer guy thinks he saw a *bird* fly into it. Some bird!"

"Could've been a low-flying plane," said the other.

"If it had been a plane it would have been spread all over the grass in a million bits," said the first man.

"Well, there's *something* in the grass. See!"

The engineer bent down to look. "It's a cassette," he said, picking it up. "Some kid must have dropped it. No label. The rain must have washed it off." He put the cassette in the cab of their truck while they started work. They finished before noon. As they drove out of the field the man who had found the cassette pushed it into the cassette player in the dash-board. It gave out a series of bleeps. "Huh! A dud!" he said. And he took it from the machine and threw it out of the window.

The repair truck had barely gone when the farmer's son came running across the field, followed by his dog. The boy picked up a stick and threw it, and the dog ran after it. But instead of bringing the stick back, the dog pawed at something on the ground, and the boy ran up to investigate.

In the grass was a cassette. He picked it up and examined it. It certainly wasn't one of his. There wasn't even anything to say what kind of music it

contained. He put it into his pocket and hurried home.

"Have you got all the music ready for the dance?" his mother asked.

"Yes," he replied. "The cassettes are all in a box in my bedroom."

He didn't remember the strange cassette he had found until he was changing his shirt to go out. He took it from his pocket, threw it on the bed, and forgot about it.

While Hound and Spike were on their way, Megatron, Starscream and Soundwave had already reached the village. Unseen by the humans, the three Decepticons watched from a high hill. Gazing across the treetops, they saw the strange structure reported by Laserbeak.

Soundwave directed his sonic detector towards it.

"CONFIRM MECHANICAL...CONFIRM ZERO MAGNETIC RESPONSE...OPERATION AND FUNCTION UNKNOWN...SUGGEST EARTHLING ENERGY SOURCE. LASERBEAK TRACE ZERO."

"These Earthlings are more advanced than we thought," said Megatron.

"That makes them dangerous," said Starscream. "Destroy them now while we have the chance."

"And lose for ever the secret of a zero magnetic energy mechanism?" cried Megatron. "Never! We will wait and watch."

*   *   *

Unaware that alien eyes watched their every move, the villagers went about their business. A car drove up to the farm. The farmer's wife went up to her son's room. She picked up the single cassette from the bed and put it into a box with a dozen others. A few minutes later the box was on the back seat of the car, being carried to the village hall.

Transformed into his jeep shape, Hound sped along the road. Spike sat in the driving seat with the map spread in front of him.

Late in the afternoon they came to a village. The village was surrounded by hills, some of them wooded, and on one hill stood a large windmill. "That must be what Laserbeak saw," said Spike.

"What is it?" asked Hound.

"It's a windmill," explained Spike. "Modern ones use wind power to pump water and generate electricity. This one was more likely used to grind corn. Let's have a closer look at the village."

Hound drove on and parked in the village square. "You wait here," said Spike. "I'll have a look around."

"Suits me," said Hound. "A snooze in the sun will be very nice after all that dashing across the countryside."

Spike followed a footpath on to one of the hills. A glint of metal caught his eye. He crept through the trees, and there in a clearing stood the giant figures of Megatron, Starscream and Soundwave.

Spike didn't wait. He raced back to Hound and called up the Autobot base.

The voice of Optimus Prime came over the radio. "What have you found?"

"The Decepticons have taken up a position overlooking the village. There's no sign of Laserbeak. The mysterious structure on the hill is something called a windmill. It's an ancient piece of old-fashioned Earth technology. All the machinery is wooden. That's why there is no magnetic response."

"Stay where you are," said Optimus Prime. "I'm on my way with a battle unit."

* * *

The battle unit was quickly formed. Optimus Prime gave his orders.

"Autobots – TRANSFORM! Cliffjumper! Ironhide! Sunstreaker! Windcharger! Ratchet, you will assume command of base until we return."

Last of all the Autobot leader transformed into his articulated truck shape. Then he led the Autobot convoy out on the road to seek and do battle with their enemies the Decepticons.

The sun had set and the moon was rising when Optimus Prime brought his force to a halt. On a hill above, the tall stone tower and outstretched arms of the windmill were black against the night sky. Spike's father, riding in the articulated truck, climbed down, and the Autobots transformed once more to robots. Optimus Prime sent a short signal, and in a few minutes they were joined by Hound and Spike.

"So, that's a windmill!" said Ironhide. "What does it do?"

Again Spike explained. "There's a breeze," said Cliffjumper. "Why doesn't it move?"

"There will be a simple brake mechanism," said Spike's father, "and gearing to adjust the sails to catch the wind, like the flaps on an aircraft wing. Our ancestors were often cleverer than we imagine."

Hound had been probing the night with his sensors. "The Decepticons are still there, but I detect no trace of Laserbeak," he reported.

The village was now a blaze of lights. People were hurrying towards the village hall, and from the hill Spike could hear strains of music.

Inside the hall a disco was in full swing. The villagers danced to the recorded music as the lights flashed and glowed on the happy faces. The disc jockey reached out to the box of cassettes as the one in the player neared the end. Without looking he slotted it in and pressed the switch... and nothing happened. He turned up the volume

and a string of electronic bleeps came from the speakers.

And the whole system exploded!

His transformer unit re-energised, Laserbeak burst out as the evil, bird-shaped robot!

The dancers screamed as the sinister creature swooped over their heads. With a crash of wood and glass Laserbeak smashed through a window and into the night sky.

The crowd fled out of the hall and into the moonlit street. Laserbeak circled overhead. His sensors detected the presence of the Decepticons, and he circled once more to get a fix on their position.

One of the villagers had run to his house. Now he came out carrying a shot-gun. In a barrage of fire Laserbeak flew towards the hills. Other armed villagers appeared, and in a moment the whole crowd was in hot pursuit of the winged robot.

Laserbeak quickly drew away from the pursuit. He saw the Decepticons among the trees and swooped in to land. Megatron and the others heard the shots and saw the flashes. As Laserbeak transformed again to a cassette and slotted into Soundwave's chest-pack, Starscream shouted: "Blast them out of existence! They dared to raise their hands against a Decepticon!"

"Hold your fire!" shouted Megatron. "*I* give the orders. And they're still out of range...at least two kilometres away!"

At the sound of distant gun shots, Optimus Prime ordered the Autobots to take up position on the hill by the windmill. The moon was bright, but it was still impossible to make out what was happening. Spike found an open door at the base of the windmill tower. He darted inside and climbed quickly up a flight of dusty wooden stairs to the top floor. He opened a window shutter, and far below he could see the shadowy figures of the villagers as they ran in the hunt for

Laserbeak. They were making straight for the woods where Megatron and the Decepticons were hidden!

Spike called down to Optimus Prime, "Stand by to create a diversion! FIRE!"

The Autobots used their energy weapons to send a stream of fire flashing towards the hidden Decepticons.

For the first time Megatron saw the Autobots on the opposite hill by the windmill. "The Autobots!" he cried. "They have taken possession of the structure reported by Laserbeak! They must know its worth! Leave the Earthlings! This is more important!"

At Megatron's command, Starscream transformed to his aircraft shape and, with Laserbeak, swept into the sky to mount an aerial attack on the Autobots. The giant figures of Megatron and Soundwave burst through the trees on the opposite side to the approaching villagers, striding across the moonlit fields, weapons blazing in a frontal attack.

In moments a fierce battle raged around the windmill.

Fusion cannons, photon rifles and blaster missiles roared and flashed. The grass and bushes on the hilltop were ripped and shredded as the giant robots struggled in hand to hand combat. Stones showered down as stray shots hit the windmill tower where Spike watched the battle from the window. Suddenly he saw a figure sprinting for the cover of the mill. It was his father. "Up here, Dad!" he shouted.

Laserbeak was circling before coming in to the attack once more when he heard Spike's voice. Going into a screaming power drive, he blasted off a missile. The missile struck just above the window, and Spike leapt back. He fell against a long lever protruding from the floor and grabbed at a loop of hanging chain to save himself. The chain moved in his hand, and with a loud groaning and rumbling the ancient wooden machinery of the mill began to move!

Megatron was first to notice the windmill sails starting to move. "The Autobots have activated the device," he shouted.

Laserbeak saw it too, but just too late. As he pressed in another attack upon the mill, he failed to notice one of the heavy sails sweeping towards him. With a splintering crash the heavy timber sail hit the mechanical bird. Pieces of wood flew in all directions. Laserbeak was undamaged, but the shock triggered the release of a missile. As

Laserbeak recovered, the missile ploughed into the ground between Megatron and Starscream, the blast hurling them to the ground.

"Stop that thing!" screamed Megatron.

Starscream knelt and aimed the null-ray projector at the mill. The mill glowed with blue light as the ray hit it, but the machinery rumbled on and the damaged sails still swung round and round in the moonlight.

"Impossible!" cried Starscream. "There is no machine which can withstand the null-ray."

From the opposite hill, the villagers watched the battle. They couldn't see much, but the roar and flash of energy weapons were clear enough. "What's happening?" they asked each other, forgetting for the moment the mysterious winged creature they had been chasing.

* * *

Again Starscream fired the null-ray.

"This thing is proof against our most powerful technology," cried Megatron. "The Autobots have learned its secret! They seek to use it against us! It must be stopped...or captured!" And the Decepticon leader again led the attack upon the Autobots.

The Autobots were being hard pressed. Already they had retreated part way down the hill. The Decepticons were close to the windmill. Soundwave suddenly cried, "DEVICE MAY NOT RESIST SHOCKWAVES...RUMBLE ACTIVATE ...OPERATION SHOCKWAVE!"

A cassette ejected and transformed into the small but powerful Decepticon, Rumble.

"I said 'STOP', not 'DESTROY'," screamed Megatron. But he was too late. Rumble's low frequency ground-wave generators were already in action. The mill began to sway as cracks ran up the height of the tower.

Spike and his father sprinted to safety, but the Decepticons were not so quick. Megatron, Starscream, Soundwave and Rumble vanished under the wreck of the huge sails and the rumble of the tower as the windmill collapsed, while Laserbeak flew in circles above the dust trying to see what had happened.

Optimus Prime called up to the flying Decepticon, "Tell Megatron we would like to stay to help, but we're rather busy at the moment."

Back on the road the Autobots transformed, and the whole convoy set off back to base.

Next day, Optimus Prime was thoughtful.

"I'm sorry about the windmill," he said. "One of our Autobot rules is that the property of the Earth people must be left unharmed. I'm also afraid that we may have been seen. The less people know of us the better."

Spike came up carrying a newspaper. "I shouldn't worry," he said. "Listen!"

"THERE ARE REPORTS FROM A REMOTE VILLAGE OF A FREAK ELECTRICAL STORM WHICH DESTROYED A WINDMILL WHICH HAD BEEN A LOCAL LANDMARK FOR OVER A HUNDRED YEARS. EVEN STRANGER IS THE REPORT OF A DISCO DANCE WHICH WAS INTERRUPTED BY THE APPEARANCE OF A 'WINGED DEMON'."

"It's a pity in a way," said Spike, "that they'll never know the true story!"

Optimus Prime is the strongest, largest and wisest of all Autobots. He is kind to all that lives, including those on Earth. When his trailer becomes the command centre, he transforms from the trailer cab to lead the Autobots in their fight against the evil Decepticons.

Hound transforms from a four-wheel-drive vehicle to the Autobot scout robot. He is brave and loyal to the Autobot cause and likes the planet Earth. Secretly, Hound would like to be human!

Sideswipe transforms from a racing car to a warrior robot. He and his twin brother, Sunstreaker, make a powerful team in the never-ending battle against the Decepticons.

Huffer transforms from a trailer cab to become the Autobot construction engineer. Although he will mutter and complain, he is a strong and reliable worker.

Jazz transforms from a racing car to the Autobot special operations agent. He takes on the dangerous missions and is clever and daring. He likes Earth and is always looking to learn more about the planet and its people.

Gears transforms from an armoured carrier to work as a transport and reconnaissance robot. Like Huffer, he likes to be miserable and find fault in everything, but he has great strength and endurance.